P336m   Peck, Robert Newton

Mr. Little

MR. LITTLE

books by Robert Newton Peck

A DAY NO PIGS WOULD DIE

PATH OF HUNTERS

MILLIE'S BOY

SOUP

FAWN

WILD CAT

BEE TREE *(poems)*

SOUP & ME

HAMILTON

HANG FOR TREASON

RABBITS AND REDCOATS

KING OF KAZOO *(a musical)*

TRIG

LAST SUNDAY

THE KING'S IRON

PATOOIE

SOUP FOR PRESIDENT

EAGLE FUR

TRIG SEES RED

BASKET CASE

HUB

MR. LITTLE

MR. LITTLE

Robert Newton Peck

Illustrated by Ben Stahl

DOUBLEDAY & COMPANY, INC., GARDEN CITY, NEW YORK

P 336m

/

Library of Congress Cataloging in Publication Data

Peck, Robert Newton.
  Mr. Little.

  SUMMARY: Greatly disappointed that the cele-
brated Miss K will not be their teacher, Finley Streeter
and Stanley Dragavich pull pranks on the new teacher
in their small town.
  [1. Humorous stories] I. Stahl, Ben, 1910–
II. Title.
PZ7.P339Mk   [Fic]
          ISBN: 0-385-13657-9 Trade
                 0-385-13658-7 Prebound
  Library of Congress Catalog Card Number 78–22347

Copyright © 1979 by Robert Newton Peck

All Rights Reserved
Printed in the United States of America
9 8 7 6 5 4

MR. LITTLE

590

P336m

chapter 1

"Hurry up, Finley."

"Okay," I said, "but I got a knot."

"A knot?" Drag wrinkled his nose.

My fingers fumbled at the knot in the string I used for a shoelace. By the way his dirty toes were tapping on the wet boards of the catwalk, I could tell that Drag was sick of waiting. Maybe he was fixing to wade across the rim of the dam without me. So I broke the string with a hard yank. I don't guess I wanted to take the shortcut, not even with Stanley Dragavich going first. But there was no way I could back off now.

"Shake a leg," Drag hollered.

"Yup," I said, peeling off my second sock, the one

with a hole in the heel near big enough to throw a rat through.

Drag was already down the rickety old stairs and up to his ankles in water at the lip of the dam. Rolling up my pantlegs, I grabbed my sneakers and socks and followed. On my right was the deep blue water of the millpond. To my left, nothing but a fall of forty feet into mist and rocks.

"Crank it up, Finley," yelled Drag.

"Here I come!"

Both of us were yelling, even though Drag was only a few feet in front of me, because the noise of the waterfall was loud this morning. As we tippytoed along the spillway, arms extended for balance, I tried not to look to the left and down over the drop. Beneath my feet, the lip of the spillway was slippery with slime, and the overflow current sucked at my shins as though it had a hanker to wash me over the falls.

"Wait!" I yelled to Drag, who was inching across faster than I could keep up. I sure wished I had *his* weight to help nail down my feet.

"You scared?" Drag hollered back.

"Nope, not me."

"I bet."

We were halfway across the top of the dam when it happened. My foot slipped on a gooey patch of green frog spit and it made my left hand sort of let loose. One sneaker and one yellow sock dropped over the falls and into the mist below. My heart jumped. I wanted to yell or run, at least to where I could grab

ahold on the back of Drag's cowboy belt. My face suddenly felt wetter than my feet.

"S'matter?" Drag yelled back.

"I dropped 'em."

"You dope."

"*Wait* for me, Drag."

The waterfall boomed noisier than ever. I wanted to go back. But then Drag would tell all the other kids and I'd probable never hear the end of it. Not for the rest of my life. They'd all claim that I was as yellow as my sock.

"Please wait up," I yelled to Drag.

He was near to all the way across. I tried to hurry and not to look to the left. Even in spite of the roar of the falls I could sort of hear my mother's voice and her usual warning whenever I left the house and headed for school: "Finley Streeter, don't you *dare* take that shortcut over the dam."

And to make matters worse, I had promised not to only this morning as I ran down the road to the fork where I always met Drag. "I won't," I had yelled over my shoulder to Mom. And now I had only one sneaker and one yellow sock. Well, at least I had hung on to the sneaker that had a regular lace. The one with the string would never be seen again.

"Hurry up, Finley."

On the far side, safe and sound, I saw Stanley Dragavich kicking the water off his dirty old feet, the same way a dog shakes dry a paw. Only fifteen more steps . . . fourteen . . . thirteen. The current sure was strong, as it had rained yesterday. Both our barrels were full-up at the house this morning. That's when I should have known that today was a sorry time to wade the dam.

Dam! Dam! Dam! I said the word over and over to myself as I took each slippery step. Here it was, the first day of school, and I sure picked a rotten way to start off September.

"Boo!" hollered Drag, trying to make me jump.

As I stopped and looked up, I saw a big grin on his full-moon face. Drag, I was thinking, you got a puny idea of what's funny. He was pulling a green sock over a pink foot.

"You're gonna fall, Finley!"

Good old Drag.

Still he had his uses. Seeing as I was Drag's pal, nobody dared to pick on me very much. Drag did. But let somebody else poke me a doozer in the belly-button and big old Drag would stomp the sides even. And on account he was so doggone hefty, whenever Stanley Dragavich would stomp on a kid, he stayed stomped.

"Made it!" I finally said.

Those wet boards of safety on the far side sure felt like heaven under my cold feet. I made it! And that, I promised myself instead of my mother, would be the last time *ever* for Finley Streeter. Never, never, never again.

"What took ya so long?"

"I dropped a sneaker and a sock. Doggone the goofy gink who ever called going this way a *shortcut*."

"I figure it is," said Drag.

"From now on," I said, "I'm going to school by way of the North Pole before I wade the dam again."

"Oh yeah?"

"Now I got one sneaker and one sock. What'll I do? I'll have to go half barefoot."

Drag chuckled. "Not if ya put a sock on one foot and your sneaker on the other."

"Swell."

"Come on, Finley. Don't just stand there and look stupid. We'll be late for school. So get yourself shod."

"Well," I told Drag, "if you'd been on time, we could have took the long way around and had a breath left over. You and your dumb shortcuts and cross-lots."

I yanked on a sock. Then, on my other foot, I pulled on my only sneaker, the one with the good lace. Knotting it, I was up and ready.

"Ha!"

"What's so funny?" I asked.

"I can hardly wait," said Drag as we left the dam behind us, scrambling up through the thornbushes that led to Elm Street and to school.

"Wait for what?"

"Yeah," said Drag. "I can't wait to notice your dear ma's face when you finally fetch yourself home."

"I sure can."

"That'll be a circus."

"For *you* maybe. Boy," I said, limping over the pebbles to keep up with Drag, "I sure wish I had another sock."

"Ya do?"

"Yeah, I sure do."

Pow! Drag's knuckles socked my shoulder.

chapter 2

"Who's he?"

As I looked to see where Drag was pointing, I saw a small man in a straw hat and a dark suit enter the front door of the school. He wiped his feet on the doormat and went inside.

"It beats me," I said.

"Maybe it's somebody's father," said Drag.

The man was a total stranger. Everyone who lived here in the town of Siberia knew everybody else. Without wiping our own feet, as our teachers said we always should (it was sort of dumb to wipe one sneaker and one sock), Drag and I charged into Siberia Central School and up the two half-flights of stairs to the top floor. The school had four rooms: two downstairs for the young kids, with two more upstairs on the second story for big kids like Drag and me. Drag was a year ahead of me in school, yet we were both assigned to Room 4—Miss Kellogg's room.

But in Room 4 there was no Miss Kellogg.

Drag and I had heard for years how great Miss Kellogg was, even though she was a teacher, and how much fun it was to be in her class. You got to go on hikes and stuff. She was the youngest and the prettiest teacher in Siberia, and her brother was an airplane pilot. But instead of Miss Kellogg, we only saw the small man in the dark suit, sitting up front behind Miss Kellogg's desk like he thought he belonged there.

"Good morning," he said softly as we entered. The rest of the kids were already seated. But something was amiss. There was no Miss Kellogg. Only the new guy.

"Hey," said Drag, "where's Miss Kellogg?"

At least he should have said "Good morning" back, and it was kind of rude not to do it, but I reckon Drag was as worked up about not seeing Miss Kellogg as the rest of us. We wanted Miss Kellogg, because every kid in town knew that she was the one teacher you were allowed to call Miss K, and she said K stood for potassium. I didn't know what potassium was, and I guessed it was something like a possum. All I cared about was having pretty Miss K for a whole year. Miss K and her beautiful smile.

The little man cleared his throat as if he almost wanted to say he was sorry that he'd come to the wrong school.

"Good morning," he said. "I am sorry to announce

that Miss Kellogg will not be with you this year, as she has decided to . . . get married."

We all let out a groan.

"Oh *no*," said Stanley Dragavich.

"Who'll be our teacher?" I asked the man.

He smiled softly. Then turning to the blackboard behind his desk, he took a new stick of chalk and clacked out a name:

Lester Little.

We also sort of mumbled "Lester Little" as though we were whispering a rumor about chicken pox. I said the name again. Lester Little. I don't want you, Lester Little, because I have waited for years to be in Miss Kellogg's room, and maybe go up in her brother's airplane, and even get a kiss on the head when I recited something like a poem that was no less than outstanding . . . and I sure didn't want to be kissed on the head, or even the *toe*, by any Lester Little. I wanted pretty Miss K.

"Boys and girls," he said, "I am Mr. Little. I am a new teacher here in Siberia, so new that I arrived in town only last evening."

Drag raised his hand, but without waiting for Mr. Little to call on him, he asked: "Do you own an airplane?"

Mr. Little smiled. "No, I'm afraid I do not."

Drag made a face.

Brother, I said silently, it's going to be a long year. No ride in an airplane, and no kisses on the head from pretty Miss Kellogg, and we probable won't even hanker to call this old turkey Mr. L.

"Are you going to live here in Siberia?" asked Betty Ann Cooper.

"Yes," said Mr. Little. "I have rented a room just down the street at Mrs. Tripper's."

"Tripper's Boarding House?"

"Yes, it's the big white house that overlooks the village green, with a long front porch that has the gingerbread trim."

"Gingerbread?" asked Drag, who was strongly in favor of food. "Can you really eat it?"

"Well," said Mr. Little, "I suppose you could, that is if you were a termite."

A few of us laughed. But not many.

"Mr. Little, can you tap dance?"

"I must admit," he said, "I can't."

"Miss Kellogg can," said Drag.

"Miss Kellogg can do everything," I said.

After I said it, I sort of had a sorry feeling somewhere in the middle of my breakfast, because Mr. Little's smile sort of faded to near match the color of his grayish-white shirt.

"Can she play a fiddle?" asked Mr. Little.

"No," said Drag.

Mr. Little smiled. "That's why life is so exciting," he said, folding his hands as he spoke to us. "We're all different, aren't we? Some folks fly an airplane, or tap dance, while other folks play a fiddle."

I asked, "Who plays a fiddle?"

Mr. Little said, "I do."

"Drag can sing," I said, and all the kids laughed.

Except for Drag who doubled his meaty fist at me.

"Which one of you is Drag?"

"Me."

"I see."

"My real name's Stanley Dragavich, but I get called Drag a lot. I don't mind."

"Can you really play the fiddle?" I asked.

"You bet. What's *your* name?"

"Finley Streeter."

"He can tap dance," said Drag, which made everybody look at my feet, including Mr. Little.

"Not that it's any of my business, Finley, but how come you're wearing only one shoe?"

"I lost it," I said.

Drag looked at me with his lips pressed together real tight as if to warn me . . . Finley Streeter, keep your big mouth shut or we'll both be in trouble. Mrs. Dragavich and my mother shared the same opinion regarding the dam.

"How did you lose your sneaker?"

Mr. Little waited patiently for my answer as if he had all day to learn the whereabouts of my missing footwear.

"A cow ate it," I said.

"She *did?*"

"Sir, we were on our way to school . . ."

"*We?*"

"Yes, sir, my sneakers and I, when I stopped to pet a cow. She looked sort of thin and a mite hungry, so I fed her a sneaker."

The class giggled.

Mr. Little raised his eyebrows. "And then you fed her one of your socks for dessert?"

"Well," I said, "I suppose it didn't happen *exactly* like that, but it sort of did happen on the way to school. I guess I sort of fancied up the story a bit. You know, about the cow."

"I understand," said Mr. Little.

"You do?"

"Much of the fun in telling a story is when you get to gussy it up some, and maybe stretch a fact into a fancy. Like the way we trim a Christmas tree. Or show with our hands how long a fish was."

The first day of school every September is always a short day, and Mr. Lester Little let us out early, a move that neither Drag nor I heartily opposed. On the way home, Drag made one of his famous observations:

"That new Mr. Little would believe just about anything you'd cook up. He'd swallow anything."

"Yeah," I said, "like a cow eats a sneaker."

chapter 3

"Where are they?"

Drag winked. "Up in the cupola. Let's go."

The cupola looked like a tiny doghouse that was roosted on the very tiptop of Drag's barn. Above the cupola was a weather vane, a black arrow to show which way the wind was blowing. Inside, the cupola was just about big enough to hold me and Drag, a pack of water-soaked Wing cigarettes that we'd found under the bleachers at the ballpark along with a book of matches that wouldn't light, a collection of bottle-caps, and several Big Little Books.

We climbed up.

First we went to the loft, using a wall ladder, and then up an iron bar until we clawed our breathless way up into the cupola. On a hot Saturday afternoon, the wee shelter in which we sat offered about as much fresh air as it did comfort (none), but Drag and I never seemed to mind. The cupola was our retreat, our hideout, where two fugitives from parental justice or chores could escape the long arm of duty or punishment. Somewhere, from a distant land that was far below, Mrs. Dragavich was calling:

"Stan-LEE! Are you up there?"

"Don't answer," whispered Drag.

We were mute as two mice. Both of us had been sternly warned that the old barn was rickety and that we should never, *ever* climb up into the loft. The cupola was even more strictly forbidden territory. We spent many a happy hour nestled in its heat, its dusty and musty filth, among the hectic hospitality of irate wasps and shy spiders. And enough old feathers to stuff a mattress for a midget.

"Well," I said to Drag as soon as we perched on a dirty rafter that was frosted with generations of sparrow manure, "where are they?"

"Close your eyes," Drag ordered.

I closed one eye, cleverly squinting from the other to watch Stanley Dragavich pry up an aging shingle, dodge a hornet, and withdraw a slim packet that was carefully wrapped in brown paper. He blew away a coating of dust.

"Okay," said Drag, "you can look."

"How many?" I asked him.

"Five," he said.

Drag, with the careful fingers that the ownership of

such treasures demanded, slowly opened the brown paper. It crackled a warning that the secrets about to unfold to us were beyond even our wildest dreams. And to think we had not one but *five* magazines in all. As I faced Drag, I tried to read upside down.

"What's the one on top?" I asked Drag.

"*Dance-Hall Cuties.*"

"Wow! Get a load of that fan dancer on the cover."

Using the caution that such a moment called for, we opened up *Dance-Hall Cuties* to the first picture story, which bore the memorable title: "Gertie's Garter." Our eyes popped upon every page, drinking in the kind of pictorial entertainment that only such revealing journalism could supply. Several pictures were missing, possibly now the guarded property of devout collectors.

The second magazine, *Midnight Models*, offered a like fare. So did the third publication, *Hotsy Harem*. We skipped over the fourth magazine, *Popular Mechanix*, in order to feast upon the fifth which, according to Al Cabrino (the high school kid whose father owned and operated Siberia's only barbershop), was the spiciest of his entire time-worn collection. As I was near to crazy about anything having to do with cowboys, I was grateful that we had saved *Bar-E Babes* for last.

Drag and I savored every yellowing page.

"Are *these* the ones we'll use?" I asked him.

"Yup," said Drag.

"All five?"

"Well, maybe not all five. I don't guess we'd get much mileage out of *Popular Mechanix*."

"I can't wait for Tuesday," I said.

"Right you are."

"How come we're going to do it to him on Tuesday?" I asked Drag.

"Last night," Drag explained, "I heard the weather report. My ma and pa listen to that same news guy every night after supper. He comes on right before Amos and Andy."

"What news guy?"

"I think his name is Old Thomas."

"He's the guy that said we'd get rain on Tuesday?" I asked Drag.

"Fair skies Monday, rain on Tuesday, and so long until tomorrow. That's the way Old Thomas sort of signs off his program."

"Which magazine will we use first?"

"I'll tell ya Tuesday," said Drag.

* * * * *

Old Thomas, or whatever his name was on the radio, had been right. Monday was sunny and fair and lasted for about a year because both Drag and I were holding our breath for good old Tuesday, and rain. It poured dogs and cats, and Mr. Little did just what Drag predicted that he'd do. On Tuesday, Mr. Little brought his black umbrella to school.

"There it is," whispered Drag.

All through arithmetic, spelling, reading, geography,

and penmanship (every oval of which I hated), we took turns staring at Mr. Little's black umbrella. If our prank was to come off as a real socko of a stunt, our timing had to be perfect. And the rain played a key role. If the sun popped out before the end of the school day, we were cooked. Our caper would really fall flat. I looked out of the window. Rain! Keep coming down, I prayed, a bit bothered by my using prayer for such an unworthy cause. But the trick we planned to play on Mr. Lester Little just *couldn't* fizzle. Or dry up.

Prior to final recess, Mr. Little always excused himself to go to the washroom in the basement, a single-seat toilet which he shared with the school's only other adult male, Mr. Epstein, the janitor. Drag and I had earlier noted that Mr. Epstein was also a "reader" of a certain type of publication similar to *Dance-Hall Cuties*. So when Mr. Little departed in the direction of the basement, Drag and I made our hurried preparations. Our prank was now primed, loaded, and itching to explode . . . as soon as Mr. Little's unsuspecting finger pulled the trigger.

"Good night, troops, and we'll see you all tomorrow," came Mr. Little's parting shot.

Free at last from the tedium of Tuesday, we all stampeded for the door, down the stairs, and waited out front with the other kids in the shelter of the overhang. Nobody, kids or teachers, seemed anxious to start home in the rain. Together we huddled. And then Mr. Little, wearing a raincoat and rubbers and carrying his tightly closed black umbrella, joined us all on the school's front stoop. Miss Johnson, Miss Hughes, and Miss O'Leary all smiled at Mr. Little who returned the smile.

"Beautiful day," said Miss Johnson.

"Yes," said Mr. Little, "for ducks."

Almost everyone, about twenty of us or more, waited for the rain to let up before dashing toward home. Drag and I, however, waited for another reason. Nonetheless, our Mr. Little seemed in no hurry to brave the downpour, chatting merrily with the other educators, exchanging tidbits of meteorology and varied opinions as to how many inches of rainfall had blessed Siberia and whether or not the local apple crop would be adversely affected.

At last the moment came! Waving a jolly good-by, Mr. Little opened his umbrella. Up it went over his unsuspecting head. And from the shelter of its silver spokes, where Drag and I had secretly stuffed it, down it fell at his feet.

A copy of *Hotsy Harem.*

chapter 4

Did we hear a gasp of horror? No.

Nor did we hear a trio of gasps from the shocked throats of Miss O'Leary, Miss Hughes, and Miss Johnson, all gray-haired spinsters who had logged many a decade in the furthering of Siberia's education, not to mention their constant dedication to molding the sterling characters of local offspring such as Stanley Dragavich and Finley Streeter.

Mr. Little laughed!

"Well," he said, "it must be Providence. What could better brighten a rainy evening at Mrs. Tripper's Boarding House than to curl up with an engaging magazine?"

Bending low, he rescued *Hotsy Harem* from the

puddle into which it had fallen, flicked off a few excess drops, and tucked it under his arm. He left smiling.

Drag looked at me. I looked back.

Both of us were utterly speechless, as though struck dumb by the sudden unity of Mr. Lester Little and a slightly harvested edition of *Hotsy Harem*. It was as if Mr. Little had opened his umbrella only to discover that he had misplaced, and found, his most coveted copy of *Popular Mechanix*.

"Well I'll be coondogged," said Drag.

Our three lady teachers said nothing, but merely stared blankly at Mr. Little's departing figure as he strode stoically through the heavy rain in the direction of Mrs. Tripper's. Their faces wore looks of approval.

"Hmmm," said Miss Johnson. "He'll do."

But a moment later, three pairs of eyes looked sternly in the direction of one pair of their former pupils, right at Drag and me. Years of suffering through frogs in desks and tacks on chairs had no doubt trained them to weather any surprise, coupled with unerring abilities of detection that would have humbled even a Sherlock Holmes. These were three teachers who could spot a culprit in a crowd or any rotten apple buried in a barrel. Their nerves had been honed to be more hardy than a railroad spike, and they had survived the annual arrivals and departures of many a Stanley Dragavich and Finley Streeter without losing their humor or sanity.

Therefore, for them to witness Mr. Little's baptism

into the fray as he collected his early bruises was no more than a natural phenomenon. Miss Johnson, Miss Hughes, and Miss O'Leary were veterans who had earned their stripes.

Drag and I bolted through the rain.

✽　✽　✽　✽　✽

Wednesday came.

With or without the help of Old Thomas, the weather turned sunny, drying out the September greenery of Siberia, and brightening the spirits of the entire school. Even those of us who expected punishment for the travesties of yesterday. It was a special day. Mr. Little came whistling to school and carrying a fiddle case as though *Hotsy Harem* had never been planted in his umbrella. And boy, could he play!

"Do you know 'Zip Coon'?" asked Drag.

"Sure do," said Mr. Little.

While our hands clapped and our toes tapped to the music, Mr. Little and his fiddle sawed off song after song. His best, according to Drag's discerning ear, was "Oh, the Moon Shines Tonight on Pretty Red Wing," a selection that Mr. Little had to play three times before we'd let him unhook the fiddle off his knee and give his arm a breather. When he played, the fiddle was never under his chin. Instead, his left foot rested on a bench, his left elbow on his thigh, and off went that fiddle like it was Saturday night in town.

He played "Juanita" and "Indian Love Call," too.

We tried to stump Mr. Little, requesting songs like

"Sweet Cider" and "Turkey in the Straw" and "Floppy-Ear Mule" . . . but that fiddle of Mr. Little's took every hurdle. We got so all-fired carried away that Drag and I stood up front, flanking our teacher at both hips, and sang "Old Brave Andy Rowley."

"Had enough?" Mr. Little asked us.

"*No!*" we yelled.

"Well I have. Best I grab myself a rest and glue my bowing arm back together."

"Awwww," we moaned.

"Besides," he told us, "it's time for drawing."

Never have I been much of an artist. In fact, I can't draw as much as a decent circle without a penny to trace around. If I attempt a horse, what I usually wind up with looks more like Luke Freemont's goat. I don't guess I'll ever be another Mr. Norman Rockwell. So I just drew a picture of a cow eating a sneaker.

Ya know, to look at some kid like Stanley Dragavich, you'd think he wouldn't be able to draw mud. But I give old Drag this much: He was the best artist in the class and maybe even the best in all of Siberia Central School. That was because he tried so hard. If a line wasn't up to snuff, old Drag would whip out his eraser and rub it out until it measured up to standard. Or until his paper tore. Usually the latter. Then he'd cuss up a storm and go back to it, even though his paper was patched all over with brown stickum tape. Sometimes he wound up with what looked less like art work and more like the town dump.

"There!" said Drag.

"What is it?"

Drag held his drawing up with both hands so's I could take a look-see.

"Gee," I said, "it's not bad."

"Thanks," said Drag.

It was a drawing of Mr. Little, foot up on the bench, fiddling his fiddle. And it really did favor Mr. Little more than a mite. Fact is, the more I looked at Drag's artwork, the more it seemed that Mr. Little actually moved and was really fiddling. You could almost hear "Zip Coon."

"Hey," I whispered, "I didn't think you liked Mr. Little."

"I don't," Drag whispered back. "We got gypped. We shoulda got Miss Kellogg."

At the suggestion of Mr. Little, we got to make frames for our drawings. All the girls in the room used a bright pink cardboard to frame their art, while we boys all got to border ours in navy blue. Then we pigged our lunches and went outside for noon recess to swing on the truck tire or to kick the football. Drag and I exchanged punts until the football went down into the sewer hole, and Mr. Epstein washed it off with his hose and a bar of brown soap.

We had to let the football dry in the sunshine. Even before it got muddy, it was heavy enough; but when that old leather pumpkin of a ball was soaking wet, it was about as much fun to kick as a tombstone. And it'd sail about as far. We thanked Mr. Epstein and then I suggested to Drag that we reward the old geezer with a present, something he'd like.

"Such as what?" asked Drag.

"*Bar-E Babes.*"

Drag punched me. "You crazy?"

That afternoon, Drag and I sure took a lot of kidding and a lot of catcalls from the rest of the guys. And even from the girls. We got joshed aplenty because some wise guy had took off our navy blue frames. Our art works, Drag's and mine, were now bordered in *pink!* Like a girl's! I couldn't figure out who'd pulled a prank like that. Nobody could have.

All the kids were out on the playground.

chapter 5

"I got one," said Drag.

The two of us were up in the cupola on top of Drag's barn, playing one of our favorite games: Horse.

"Okay," I said, "fire away."

"What's the name of Hopalong Cassidy's horse?"

"That's a cinch," I said. "Topper. Now it's my turn. How about Gene Autry's?"

"Champion."

"Right. Your turn."

Drag scratched his backside, something he always did whenever he was trying to think up a real zinger. "What's the name of the white horse Buck Jones rides?"

"Silver," I said. "How about Tom Mix's?"

Drag said, "Tony."

"Yup," I said.

"Roy Rogers's?"

"Trigger," I said, "and his dog's name is Bullet. Who's the Lone Ranger's?"

"Silver," said Drag. "Same as Buck's. I can't think of any more."

"I can."

"Yeah, but it ain't your turn. But go ahead if you think you got a stumper."

"Okay," I said, "what's the name of War Admiral's sire?"

Drag wrinkled his nose. "I give up."

"Man o' War; and War Admiral's son is Seabiscuit."

"Here's my last one," said Drag. "If you think you're so smart, what's the name of Ken Maynard's horse, or Tim McCoy's?"

"I don't know," I said.

"Me neither," Drag sadly admitted.

"That's not fair," I said.

"How come?"

"Well, you're supposed to know the answer to your own question. And I already know the answer to *this* one."

"Shoot."

"How about Tonto's?"

"Aw, that's a snap. Scout."

"I can't think of any more."

"Neither can I. Besides, I'm sort of thinking about something else besides horses, if you wanna know the truth."

Reaching into the hip pocket of his faded old brown corduroy pants, Drag pulled out a buckeye and started to shine it, rubbing the horse chestnut up and down between his nose and cheek.

"Finley, we gotta get even."

"You mean with Mr. Little?"

"Yeah," said Drag, "because he's the one who put pink frames on our pictures. He made us two into a couple of goats."

"If you ask me," I said, "you and I started it, when we snuck the copy of *Hotsy Harem* into Mr. Little's umbrella. And then *he* settled the score with *us*."

"Are you on *his* side?"

"Nope," I said.

"You sure sound like it."

"Well, I just think that Mr. Little is a good sport. He can take a joke and he can dish it out."

"I can dish it out, too," said Drag.

"You're not fixing to make trouble for Mr. Little, are ya?"

"First off," said Drag, stuffing the buckeye back into his pocket, "we gotta find his weak spot."

"Suppose he doesn't have one?"

Drag snorted. "Everybody's got a weak spot. You know, like a boxer who has what they call a glass jaw. I read that in *Ring* magazine."

"So you're bent on finding out where Mr. Little hides his weak spot."

"Sure thing," said Drag, "and then I'll know how to attack."

"Mr. Little might be tougher than you figure."

"Him? He don't look tough to *me*."

Drag picked up a pigeon feather and blew it up into the air. As it started to fall, I blew on it, too. Between his blowing and mine, we kept that old feather buzzing around in circles up under the roof of the cupola. Sure was fun. Finally the little feather sailed out through a slit between the slats and floated off into the sky, headed toward the freedom of rural Siberia.

"It got away," said Drag.

"Did you ever wonder what it was like to be a feather?" I asked Drag.

"Nope. Have you?"

"Lots of times. I wonder if that old feather just sort of got sick of playing with us and then up and decided it would soar off into space. Maybe feathers have dreams of flying, just like kids."

"Do you ever dream of flying, Fin?"

"Almost every night. Or at least once a week. What do you dream about mostly?"

"Food," said Drag.

"The best dream I ever had was about Miss Kellogg."

"Yeah?"

"I had on a yellow bowtie. I dreamed that I was a grown-up man, six feet tall, and that I was Miss Kellogg's boyfriend. I drove right up to the schoolhouse in a Packard roadster that was painted bright yellow. And then out pranced Miss Kellogg in a yellow polka-dot dress, and we went down to the Crick and had a picnic."

"With mustard?" Drag asked me.

"Mustard?"

"Yeah," said Drag. "Everything else in your dream is yeller, so you must of had hotdogs and mustard."

"Maybe we did. But one of the best parts of the dream was when I carved K into the bark of a birch tree, and then outlined it with a heart."

"Some dream."

"Boy, it sure was. I even told Miss Kellogg that I had to go away, but I'd be back and then we'd get married in the Methodist church."

"What happened next?"

"Miss Kellogg wanted me to kiss her."

"I bet you were too chicken."

"Well, I guess I sort of was at first."

"Then what?"

"Right after I asked her to marry me and be Mrs. Finley Streeter, she told me that I had to give her a ring, to sport up her hand."

"And you didn't have a ring."

"I sure did! Ya see, I was smoking a cigar in the dream, so I just slipped the paper cigar-band right off the cigar and put it around Miss Kellogg's finger. Then I kissed her."

"Wow!" whispered Drag. "On the cheek?"

"Nothing doing. Her lips were close to mine, drawing closer and closer, and as she closed her eyes . . ."

"Just like in the picture show."

"Her lips tasted soft and sweet, sort of like eating strawberry ice cream that was part melted on a hot day."

"Gee," said Drag, "and to think of all those nights I wasted."

"Wasted on what?" I asked him.

"On dreaming about jellybeans."

chapter 6

"Fin!"

The pebble clinked against the glass of my bedroom window, and I heard it dribble down the roof and into the rain gutter.

"Hush up," I told Drag, "or you'll wake up my father. If you do, then Heck won't have it."

I heard Drag's whisper come out of the darkness. He was standing in the moonlight right under the old apple tree in our side yard. "Hurry up."

"Here I come."

As I carefully backed out my bedroom window, good old Drag threw another stone. Twack! I felt it sting my butt. Turning around, as I crept along the roof of our house, I could look down and see him grin up at me. Leaning out over the roof corner, I grabbed the limb of the apple tree, feeling the knotty bark under my hands, and swung easily to the ground.

"Did you bring a flashlight?" I asked.

"Naw," said Drag. "There's a full moon, and we can scamper down and back without nobody seeing us."

"Yeah," I agreed. "Maybe a flashlight might just give us away."

"I don't guess we aim to get caught," said Drag.

"How come?"

"On account we might run into old Mayburn, and Pa already switched me for playing the magazine prank on Mr. Little. I sure don't hanker for a second dose."

"Yeah," I nodded.

Mayburn Hurley was Constable of Siberia, and the only uniformed defender of local ordinance, as well as peace and order. Very little happened in Siberia, before dark or after, that Mayburn didn't know all about —where it was happening and sometimes even why. He was a big bull of a man, and some folks said that Mayburn weighed a meal or two beyond three hundred pounds. He was too strong to be mean. You'd be hard put to determine exactly which hours Mayburn Hurley was "on duty," or when he was off.

Drag and I went over the shed roof behind the old Sheldon house and ducked through a loose slat in the fence. Without giving much respect to domestic tranquility, my hand sort of let loose of the board. It went *bang* back into place.

A light went on!

"Run," hissed Drag.

We ran.

Drag kicked an empty gas can and stubbed his toe, letting out a curse that echoed off into the night, as well as creating a clanking for all Siberia to hear.

"Who's out there?" a voice asked.

Again we ran.

I knew we were somewhere close to the center of downtown Siberia, such as it was, in the alley behind a row of stores. Not too far from McMurtree's Laundry because the strong smell of soap powder and cleaning fluid was smarting my nostrils, causing my eyes to leak. For a moment, I couldn't see.

In a hurry, I bumped smack into Drag, climbing halfway up the back of his chubby leg.

"Watch it, Streeter."

"Sorry," I said.

"It's this way," said Drag.

I squinted into the dark. "I'm all turned around. Everything looks so different."

"Do your eyes feel sort of funny?"

"Yeah, do yours?"

"There must have been some gas in the can we knocked over. My sneakers feel kind of wet," said Drag.

"We gotta find Mrs. Tripper's."

"Just follow me," Drag said. "I can see better in the dark than a hungry cat."

We raced around a corner. When my hip knocked

the lid off a garbage can, it fell with a loud clang, and then rolled through the grit and into a bunch of what smelled like paint cans. I never thought the noise would quit, but it finally did.

"You run like a blind mule," said Drag.

"Come on," I said to Drag, "or we'll never get to Tripper's Boarding House."

Again we sprinted. A dog started to bark, so we ran faster, spilling ourselves and varied stacks of rubbish, much of which rattled in our wake. My shin whacked against the edge of a wooden step which caused me to let out a whoop of discomfort. Another light went on. Out of breath, we stopped to let our hearts pump back to normal.

"Look for a clothesline," whispered Drag.

"You sure we can find it?"

"We gotta find it. Stewy Ordway told me that Mr. Little does his own wash, every Monday after school, and hangs it out back of the boarding house where he lives."

"Well," I said, "today's Monday."

"At the rate we're going, we'll be near to Tuesday noon before we get ahold of what we're after."

"Let's go."

"Okay."

Stumbling and tripping, we ran through the alley, knocking over various heaps of this and stores of that, all of it without identity . . . causing the electric bill in more than one second floor to increase as we worked our way through nocturnal Siberia.

"Keep looking for the clothesline," said Drag.

We never did find the clothesline. Instead, as we raced through the darkness, the clothesline found us. Something caught me and Drag, just below our chins, and for one wild and painful second I thought my head was cut off. From the neck down, I kept on running, landing flat on my fanny. That was enough hurt for any kid, but when Drag landed on top of me, it was hard to say where the pain stopped and the agony began.

"Off," I wheezed.

When I heard Drag try to swallow, I figured his throat felt about as sorry as mine. He sure was one heavy hunk of horse meat.

"What was that?" I finally gargled out.

We got up, Drag holding his neck while I held mine. It hurt like all fury.

"A clothesline," said Drag.

"Yeah, but *whose?*"

Squinting into the darkness, I could make out the large gingerbread residence known by every soul in Siberia as Tripper's Boarding House. As I stumbled around in the dark, eyes smarting and neck throbbing, a very wet object slapped me in the face. A wet shirt. Next on the line, several pairs of wet socks. I looked for what might have been a yellow one, but no luck.

"Here," I heard Drag whisper.

"What is it?"

"Fin, we just struck gold."

Slowly, I groped my way along the clothes rope to

where Drag was removing an article of wet clothing. He unpinned a clothespin.

"Stewy Ordway was right," whispered Drag.

"About what?"

"Lester Little *does* do his own wash. Better yet, Stewy was right about Mr. Little's tag on all his clothes."

Drag held up a wet pair of undershorts under a crack of light from a window. Then I saw what Drag had seen and it made me smile, hurt throat and all. Our trip had paid off. Drag and I had really struck gold. There, on the wet undershorts, I saw the name:

Lester Little.

chapter 7

Mr. Little cleared his throat.

"Troops," he said, "as you know, on Wednesday of next week there is *no school.*"

We all cheered, except Drag.

"Here in Siberia, next Wednesday means Founder's Day, the day set aside each year to honor the citizen who was Siberia's folk heroine and first settler, over two hundred years ago. Now, as I am a newcomer to Siberia, I can learn more about this legendary subject from you than you can from me. Who'd like to tell us the name of Siberia's famous founder?"

Arlidge Turner raised his hand. "Her name was Samantha Brainlee Westcox."

"I believe that is correct," said Mr. Little, "and it's my understanding that she was the sole survivor of an

Indian massacre that took place here in Siberia over two hundred years ago. That is why, as I'm sure all of you already know, there is a life-size granite statue of Samantha Brainlee Westcox commanding the very hub of your village green."

Drag yawned.

I didn't, but I was bored. Every kid in Siberia had heard the saga of Samantha Brainlee Westcox over and over, year in and year out, from every single teacher and from both parents. Even at Sunday school. So hearing it again was about as exciting to me as an opening night for a new telephone booth.

Founder's Day meant just one thing to me, and it had nothing whatsoever to do with either Indians or Samantha Brainlee Westcox. It only meant a day of no school. No geography, no penmanship, and no Lester Little.

"Are they still hid?" I whispered to Drag from a corner of my mouth.

"Sure are."

"Maybe somebody will find 'em."

"Nope, nobody will. You and I are the only ones who ever climb up in the cupola. And if old Little goes snooping around town to look for his missing undershorts, up in our cupola would be probable the last place a body would think to search."

Mr. Little droned on and on, saluting the courage of Samantha Brainlee Westcox and the wit she employed to escape with her auburn locks unshorn by knife or by tomahawk. "And so," explained Mr. Little, "your four teachers here at Siberia Central School have decided to make this coming Founder's Day an even more special event."

"Brother," sighed Drag.

"This year," said Mr. Little, "we are going to present a pageant to more or less relive the true experience of Samantha Brainlee Westcox, the demise of her family, and her ultimate escape."

"She got away on a raft," said Ernestine Keefer.

"I believe that's the tune," said Mr. Little.

"And," continued Ernestine, "she paddled across what is now our millpond, just above the dam, rowing all the way to safety on the far shore."

"Marvelous," said Mr. Little. His hands looked as if they were just about to applaud Ernestine's recitation.

"It was so cold here that first winter," said Katie Bly, "that she went a mite snow-crazy. So when she grew up, she named the place Siberia."

As old Drag looked in my direction, his face made a smirk, telling me how sick he was of Siberia's history and Miss Westcox's epic experience.

"Now," said Mr. Little, "for the exciting news you have so patiently awaited. Our pageant will re-enact the historic episode, followed by a picnic and hoedown. In the afternoon, a baseball game between our two amateur ballclubs, the Siberia Tigers and the Siberia Huskies . . . with ice cream and lemonade and all sorts of goodies."

Drag's face brightened a bit.

"Playing the parts of the attacking Indians will be you lads of Siberia," said Mr. Little, "and the role of

Chief Sitting Duck will be filled by our local peace officer, Mayburn Hurley."

This was getting good, I thought. It would take the feathers off a dozen turkeys to cover even *half* of Mayburn Hurley.

"Miss O'Leary has consented to play the piano, in costume of course, and I will accompany her on the fiddle. The brave colonists who were so brutally massacred will be handled by the other classes."

Turning his head so that Mr. Little could not observe, Drag tongued his gum and blew a bubble. It popped rather quietly, leaving a pink mess over much of his face.

Agatha Zerby raised her hand. "Who gets to be the star? I mean who's going to play the part of Samantha Brainlee Westcox?"

Here we go again, I thought. Agatha Zerby had the longest and yellowest hair compared to any other kid in Siberia. Each and every Christmas pageant we put on meant that the angel was always Agatha Zerby. Last year, Agatha was Heidi; and the year before, the play should have been entitled *Agatha Zerby of Sunnybrook Farm*.

Mr. Little's face lit up like a lantern.

"Ah!" he said. "Now for the sweetest surprise of all. You'll never guess who has been chosen to be Samantha Brainlee Westcox. Can you guess?"

"Agatha Zerby," we all moaned.

"Excellent idea!" said Mr. Little, watching Agatha smile with the confidence of established stardom. "And perhaps *next* year, Agatha *can* play the part."

Drag's face went blank. So did mine. Not to mention the look of absolute shock on the face of Agatha Zerby who considered herself Siberia's answer to Shirley Temple.

"Who?" we all asked.

"Someone you all know," said Mr. Little, giving us his shy little smile, the one he usual saves for dessert.

"Who's it going to be?" we demanded.

"Samantha Brainlee Westcox will be played by . . . Miss Kellogg."

Miss Kellogg! Our very own Miss K, a thought that spurred my yearning heart to leap like a goosed gazelle.

"Yes," said Mr. Little. "We heard only last week that she and her husband were planning to come back to Siberia for Founder's Day. Knowing her popularity, we thought it would be only fitting and proper for Miss Kellogg to play Samantha."

"But her name isn't Miss Kellogg any more," said Stewy Ordway. "Is it?"

"No," said Mr. Little, "it is not. But yet we took a liberty or two in printing up the handbills and posters, explaining to Miss Kellogg of course why we wished to use her former name that was so familiar to everyone here in Siberia."

"Miss Kellogg," I slowly and reverently exhaled. Suddenly our Founder's Day pageant became a much more enticing event.

"That's not *all* the news," said Mr. Little.

I wondered what could possible be news to upstage Miss Kellogg's dramatic comeback.

"As you know, the statue in our village green," said Mr. Little, "has been so badly battered and buffeted by weather that the granite has pitted in places, and its color has clouded to a dingy gray. Well, the Stalwart Monument Company down in Johnson City has offered, for no extra charge, to borrow Samantha to rebuff her so she looks good as new."

I was thinking about Miss Kellogg, not paying too much attention to Mr. Little's accounting of revised statuary.

"On Founder's Day," he said, "Mayor Eugene Puggett will unveil a shiny new Samantha Brainlee Westcox for all of Siberia to see."

chapter 8

"Lavender," I said as I laughed.

"Yeah," said Drag, "they sure are."

As we sat up in Drag's cupola, the two of us looked at each other and exchanged a stretchy grin. Near us, on a pair of dusty splinters that sprouted from a rafter, hung Mr. Little's undershorts.

"How come they're lavender?"

Drag smiled his crooked smile. "That," he said, "is what I figured out."

"So tell me."

"It's like this, Fin. By accident, my mother washed Pa's long red underwear in the same tub with some white stuff once. Ma said the color ran, whatever that means."

"What's it mean?"

"Well, I guess some of the red in Pa's longies sneaked into the other stuff. That turned the white clothes sort of pink."

"Maybe that's what happened to Mr. Little's undershorts," I said.

"Yeah," said Drag. "The way I figure it, old Lester Little pulled a boner and washed his white stuff in with a purple shirt."

"And that's how come his undershorts are sort of lavender?"

"That's how come. At least, that's *my* guess."

I snapped my fingers. "Now I recollect. About a year back, you had pink socks all winter, into spring, and right up to barefoot."

Drag nodded. "I sure did."

I looked at the lavender undershorts, dry and stiff and wrinkled, hanging before us in the half-light of the cupola. And it was still in place, in plain sight, the little name tag proclaiming the lavender underwear as the property of Lester Little.

"Perfect," I said.

"Yeah," said Drag, "on account we'll just scamper to school right early some morning, before anyone else gets there . . ."

"And while old Mr. Epstein is down in the basement with his copies of *Hotsy Harem*. . . ."

"That'll be our chance," said Drag, "to get to the bulletin board in the downstairs hall and pin up Mr. Little's undershorts."

"Or run 'em up on the flagpole," I said, "instead of Old Glory. Then we can recite our Pledge of Allegiance to the underwear." I giggled at the thought.

"Hey," said Drag, "you know the roller map that pulls down in our room?"

"Yeah."

"Well, we could glue his undershorts to the blackboard, and then pull down the map. Then when he rolls *up* the map, there they are!"

"I got a better idea," I said.

"Maybe so and maybe no."

"My idea has to do with Wednesday."

"You mean on Founder's Day?"

"Yup," I said. "It's a pip."

"Like what? Part of the pageant?"

"Sort of."

"When big old Mayburn Hurley gets all gussied up like Chief Sitting Duck, it'd be snazzy if he'd wear Lester's lavender shorts."

"You gotta be kidding, Dragavich. Mayburn Hurley could barely stuff his big toe into Mr. Little's undershorts. Can't you just see Mayburn trying to yank this little pair of briefs up over *his* bulk. He's got a bottom that would fill a barn door."

Drag and I were laughing so hard we could hardly hang on to our perch in the cupola. Even the lavender undershorts seemed to be shaking with the fun of it. Either that or trembling at the thought of stretching to cover even the left half or the right half of Mayburn Hurley.

"Okay," said Drag, "what's your idea?"

I laughed again, just picturing in my mind who'd be wearing Mr. Little's lavender shorts on Founder's Day, and why. "Boy," I told Drag, "this is about the best idea my brain ever hatched."

"Well, what is it?"

"Yessir," I said, "there is one perfect place for Mr. Little's lavender undershorts, and I *don't* mean on Mr. Little."

"Doggone you, Finley. Open up."

"Best I whisper it."

"Is it *that* big of a secret?" asked Drag.

"Well, it probable won't be if I tell you, on account you'll have to blab it all over Siberia."

"No, I won't."

"Honest?"

"Honest," said Drag. "I won't tell."

"Cross your heart and hope to burp in church?"

Drag crossed his heart, professing his eagerness to relieve gastric distress on the forthcoming Sabbath.

"Okay," I said, "I guess I can trust ya."

"Thanks," said Drag with a smirk.

My lips close to Drag's soiled ear, I softly disclosed exactly where we could position Mr. Little's lavender undershorts. I explained how we'd do it, and even how people who saw Mr. Little's shorts would darn near jump out of theirs. It sure would be more fun than our *Hotsy Harem* prank.

Drag gave a grin. "It'll serve him right."

"And," I continued, "we make sure that the undershorts are inside out."

"What for?"

"So," I explained to Stanley Dragavich, "his name tag will show."

"And they'll know whose shorts they are."

"You got it," I said.

"Finley, old bean, I gotta hand it to ya on this one."

"Ain't it a beaut?"

"Certainly is. We'll really get even."

Drag gave me a friendly clap on the back. It darn near made me lose my balance, and for a moment my whole body went wet with sweat.

"We'll need some shears," I said.

"And some thread."

"A needle, too."

"When 'll we do it?" Drag asked.

"Tuesday night."

"Best we use our flashlights this time."

I said, "Best we don't."

"How come?"

"If old Mayburn Hurley catches us, Pa will be so fired up, I won't be able to sit for a week."

"Yeah," said Drag, "likewise for my old man. My bottom still stings."

"We gotta be more careful than a fat dog at a flea circus."

chapter 9

"Places!" yelled Mrs. Puggett.

It was Tuesday, after school. But instead of being free to have fun until choretime, we all had to march down Elm Street to the bank of the millpond and rehearse the Founder's Day pageant. Miss Johnson, Miss Hughes, and Miss O'Leary were also on hand to herd us all in more or less the right direction. At least we didn't have to recite any lines as we did in the plays at school.

Drag and I were Indians.

The pageant's director, the one who was telling everyone where to go and what to do, was Mrs. Eugene Puggett, the mayor's wife and also an enormous woman. She was Constable Mayburn Hurley's sister. Everyone in Siberia knew about Mrs. Puggett's love of the theater. She never missed a movie, a play, or even a minstrel show. Small wonder that Mrs. Puggett was selected to direct the Founder's Day pageant to honor Samantha Brainlee Westcox; and starring our former teacher, the former Miss Kellogg.

"Places, everyone!"

Mrs. Puggett wore sunglasses. And riding breeches, boots, a tweed jacket with a blazing orange scarf, with an orange beret atop her sort-of-orange hair. Around her neck was a whistle; her hand held a small cheerleader's megaphone and several loose pages of stage directions. She was certainly Siberia's version of what we all imagined to be a movie producer from Hollywood.

"Keep back, all you Indians," Mrs. Puggett bellowed into her megaphone, which was aimed at Drag and me. "All you colonists come and pretend you're camping for the night."

"What do we do?" asked Stewy Ordway.

"Just camp," said Mrs. Puggett. "We'll work out the details as we go along. Now, seeing as Miss Kellogg won't be with us until tomorrow, just pretend that *I'm* Samantha Brainlee Westcox, which means I'm the little girl in the family of campers."

Drag snorted. "Pretending that big babe is a little girl is about as easy as believing a moving van is a roller skate."

I snickered.

"Quiet, you Indians. We don't yet know that you are waiting for us in ambush."

"Which bush?" said Drag.

Again I checked back a giggle.

"Now then," hollered Mrs. Puggett as she consulted her papers, one of which blew from her fingers and into the pond. It floated lazily toward the brink of the dam. "All we settlers are busy making supper, so just gather around me in a circle and pretend I'm a campfire. We are totally unaware that at this very moment the Westcox family is being spied upon by murderous redskins."

Drag let out a loud war whoop.

Miss Johnson shot both of us a warning glance, as if to tell us that our first whoop was our last. I smiled at Miss Johnson and she winked back.

"Where's the raft?" asked Mrs. Puggett.

Miss O'Leary came forward. "It's back in the school basement. Mr. Epstein's working on it so it will be ready by tomorrow."

"Very well," sighed Mrs. Puggett. "All of you pretend that *I'm* a raft, and I'll make believe that I'm all set to launch."

Drag and I watched Mrs. Puggett flit from one task to the next, frantically pretending to be a raft, a campfire, and Samantha Brainlee Westcox, dropping hints and papers as she leaped from position to position, and punctuating each stage direction with a blast on her whistle. She also said "Ready to roll" and "Quiet on the set" as well as an "Action" or two.

Drag and I started a wrestling match in the bushes, as there wasn't much else to do while the campers were camping. But our fun was cut short when our teacher broke us apart.

"Boys," said Mr. Little, "stop acting like a couple of wild Indians." And then his face added his funny little smile.

"Sorry," I said.

Drag didn't say anything. He just sort of scowled at Mr. Little for spoiling our fight. I was sort of glad about his spoiling it, on account I was on the bottom and big old Drag was the next body up. That kid sure was a load.

"Now," said Mrs. Puggett, "the colonists all sing a song around the campfire, as Miss O'Leary plays the piano and Mr. Whatever-His-Name-Is . . ."

"Mr. Little."

"Yes, of course . . . and Mr. Little plays his fiddle."

The campers then sang "Keep the Home Fires Burning."

"Nice," said Mrs. Puggett to her megaphone. "And so, as our hardy little band of unsuspecting settlers settle down for the night, the Indians creep forward and . . ."

Nothing happened.

"Forward, you creeps," said Mrs. Puggett, waving to Drag and me and the rest of our tribe. "I meant to say . . . you Indians."

Drag let out another war whoop, just as we charged into the circle of kids who were lying in the mud on the shore of the millpond, pretending to be comfortably asleep.

"Muskets fire," said Mrs. Puggett, looking around in a twist of confusion. "Who is supposed to fire the musket?"

"I am," said Reggie Mott.

"Well, where *is* it?"

"Home, over our fireplace. My mother said that I wasn't allowed to bring it to school today. Maybe tomorrow, if I don't wet my bed any more."

Mrs. Puggett didn't say anything. She merely withdrew a hanky from her pocket and patted her face. "I see," she finally told Reggie. "Well then, we'll all just have to pretend that I'm a musket." She drew a breath. "Bang!" she hollered.

"Can I get shot?" asked Drag.

"*May* I get shot?" insisted the musket.

Drag said, "May I?" and then, without waiting for an answer, Drag screamed in make-believe agony, hands clutching his heart. Over he fell, kicking and rolling in the mud. Drag never minded dirt very much. You get used to a lot of it if you're a kid who hangs around a cupola.

After a full minute of thrashing, with both legs kicking, Drag finally "died."

"Time," said Mrs. Puggett, "for little Samantha Brainlee Westcox to escape the massacre. Bravely she run to the raft." Mrs. Puggett broke into a fast waddle which, for her, was twice the speed of her slow waddle.

I continued to "tomahawk" the settlers.

"Here go I," said Mrs. Puggett, "across the pond to the haven of a distant shore"—she gestured across the water toward the dam—"to escape the horrors of knife and tomahawk, and to found a settlement later known as . . . Siberia!"

We all clapped our hands. Not really for the heroic escape of Samantha Brainlee Westcox, but because our rehearsal had mercifully ended. And then we all clapped even harder for one more reason:

Mrs. Puggett turned her ankle on a wet pebble and stumbled into the pond.

chapter 10

Even though the night was pitch dark, I lay wide awake, lying flat on my back in my bed and listening to my father cough and flush the toilet.

Hurry, I thought.

Once again our house was finally quiet, and all Streeters were asleep except for me, so I rolled off my bed. Sneakers, pants, and shirt composed my wardrobe. With my bedroom window up, I crossed the roof, climbing down the apple tree and jumping into the dust below. I made it through the back hedge to Drag's house.

"Drag!" I whispered.

There was no answer. Doggone you, Dragavich, wake up. Great! Here I am all ready to leg it into town, and old reliable Stanley Dragavich is upstairs asleep, curled up cozy, probably with a dumb smile on his face.

"*Drag!*" I whispered louder.

Still no answer. Well, I thought, I'd just have to caper it alone. It was my idea to begin with. My hand felt the shears in my pocket, along with a pile of pins. I had ruled out using needle and thread. Pins were perfect. With a shrug of my shoulders, leaving Drag to his dreams, I turned toward his barn. Funny, but the door was ajar.

My spine feeling like gooseflesh, I went in. But then I must have walked smack into a spider web, because my face was all sticky and crawlsome, so much that it was all I could do not to let out a scream. Before I could even wonder how many spiders were on me, I heard a noise.

"Who is it?" I hissed into the darkness, asking so quietly that the words were too faint even for my own hearing.

My knees were knocking. So I darn near *flew* up the wall ladder. I cracked my knee on a rung and almost lost my balance. Then I crept along the loft on hands and toes, feeling the seeds of hay beneath my fingers and smelling what little was left of summer, even though the barn was loaded up.

Now, I thought, to shinny up the pole and get Mr. Little's undershorts. Then I heard a low voice!

There sure was *somebody* in this barn besides me, and the spiders and I were scared to find out *who*. But I sure wasn't alone in the dark of that loft. My nose sort of got smarted as I bumped into the iron bar that was part of the main structure, the same black iron rod that rose straight up to the top of the cupola. I'd be safe up there.

Up the bar I went. But inside the grip of my hands, I felt the iron twitch, and sort of tingle a bit. Good grief, I thought, whoever it is in the barn is up in the cupola, waiting for me. A burglar or a thief or maybe an escaped criminal from the lunatic hospital.

Smush!

It landed on me, and we both tumbled down onto the hard boards of the loft floor. The person moaned. And I moaned, too. A flashlight stabbed its ray into my eyes, and I was almost blinded because it was so close to my face. Whoever held that flashlight sure had a trembling hand.

"Finley?"

"Yeah. Drag?"

"Good gosh almighty, you darn near stopped my heart. I thought some tramp had sneaked into the barn and was coming up in the cupola to commit mayhem."

My heart was pounding louder than a tom-tom. Drag's flashlight was still shining into my eyes which caused me to squint. I could barely make out Drag's head.

"Did you get Mr. Little's undershorts?"

"Sure did. And look, Fin." Drag shined his light on the cloth. "His shorts still look lavender, even at night."

"Swell," I said. "Here, I'll take 'em."

Out of the barn we went, Drag with the flashlight and me with Mr. Little's undershorts. We headed across the empty lot toward the center of town. I told Drag to turn off the flashlight before big old Mayburn Hurley spotted us and got his paws on our collars. But there's something about carrying a flashlight at night. Your hand just keeps flicking it to see if it still works.

Drag's light went on off on off on off.

"I got an idea," said Drag.

"Like what?"

"Let's take the shortcut over the dam. I reckon it'll save us a good ten minutes, both for coming into town and again going back."

"Nothing doing," I told him.

"You're too chicken, Finley?"

"Right," I cackled back, "but at least I aim to be a *dry* chicken, and one that ain't busted up on a pile of rocks."

"Chicken," said Drag.

"Ya know," I said to Drag as we stood at the narrow footpath that led to the dam's nearside catwalk, "there's something stuck in my craw."

"What?"

"Well," I said, "it's what Mr. Little said in school just yesterday. He said that we often come to a place where a brain stops working and a fool starts."

"So?"

"For me, Drag old boy, that particular place is on the near side of the dam. If'n you cotton to wade the dam on a dark night, I won't stop ya. But I sure will miss ya when you're dead."

Drag sort of swallowed. "I ain't scared."

"Okay," I told Drag, "so you're not scared. I'm not either."

"Then you'll wade the dam?"

"Nope."

"How come?"

"Because," I said, "just once in our lives, you and me oughta follow our brains instead of our bowels."

Drag scratched his behind, and nodded.

We went around the dam by taking the road bridge, the safe way, and I sure wasn't sorry. The village green was purple with dark shadows of black. Above us, no spot of a moon. We crept along, keeping low and out of sight. Then, as the moon suddenly popped through a hole in the clouds, we saw somebody standing very still, under a big gray covering. Like a sheet.

"Is that *her?*" asked Drag. He should have said *she.*

"I sure hope so," I stuttered.

Climbing up on Drag's beefy shoulders, I crawled up under the sheet. Actually the cover was sort of heavy and damp, like a tarp, but underneath . . . there she was! In granite—Samantha Brainlee West-cox, all newly buffed and polished by the Stalwart Monument Company, ready to be unveiled tomorrow by Mayor Eugene Puggett. I couldn't see her but she sure felt smooth.

"Hand me his undershorts," I whispered down to Drag. "Okay, now the shears."

Carefully, working under the dark of the tarp, I cut Mr. Little's lavender undies until they snugged around

Samantha's cold hips. Next I added pin after pin until the shorts stayed up in place. I made sure the "Lester Little" name tag was on the outside.

"Hurry," said Drag.

I still was standing on his shoulders when I heard a deep voice. It sounded like Mayburn Hurley. Light flickered beneath me, and I figured it wasn't from Drag's flashlight. Oh no!

"Sonny boy, whatcha up to?"

"Nothing," said Drag. "Just lookin' for night crawlers to go fishin' with. Honest."

"That why ya got the light?"

"Uh . . . yes, sir."

"But you don't have a pail," said Mayburn.

"No," said Drag. "I forgot it."

"What's your name, boy?"

"Finley Streeter," said Stanley Dragavich.

Below me, I heard Mayburn Hurley collar Drag. And then I felt Drag walk out from under my feet. I grabbed a quick hold, my arms around Samantha Brainlee Westcox, and hung on as still as a real statue.

"Say," said Constable Hurley's voice, "this tarp is loose. Best I tighten her up a tug or two before a wind comes up and blows off the cover." The ropes went tight around the big drapery, binding me closer to Samantha than I had ever planned. I couldn't budge. And I didn't dare to holler for help.

It sure was one long night.

chapter 11

I must have fallen asleep.

It was certainly the only way I could have fallen, as big old Mayburn Hurley had roped Samantha Brainlee Westcox and Finley Streeter tightly together, worse than an Indian ropes a cowboy to a tree.

But now I was awake, and there wasn't one bone or one muscle in my entire body that didn't ache. And if the statue of Samantha was hard, I felt even harder. To make matters worse, there was less air to breathe under that heavy old tarp than there was up in Drag's cupola. Somewhere a band was playing, people were cheering, and the parade was marching closer and closer. It was morning. I had to get out of this mess. But how?

"Help!" I hollered.

But as I was wedged up under the tarp, no one would probable hear. I could barely hear myself. Voices came closer and closer.

"Up here!" I yelled again.

Some women were talking. I didn't recognize any of the voices, but I sure knew the subject of their conversation. They all talked at once:

"Did you hear the awful news?"

"No. What happened?"

"The little boy who was lost."

"What boy?"

"The poor little Streeter boy."

"He disappeared sometime during the night and the Streeters are absolutely frantic. And the Volunteer Fire Department's over by the dam. They fear he might have drowned."

"Mary Streeter must be near out of her mind."

"Well, wouldn't *you* be, if *your* child was missing?"

"Here comes Verna."

"Say," said the new voice, "I just heard that it isn't the little Streeter boy that they're searching for."

"Who then?"

"It's the Dragavich boy."

"No, because he was found."

"Where?"

"Constable Hurley found him late last night, and *he* somehow thought it was the Streeter child. Woke the Streeters up and told them he'd found Finley. And then the Streeters told Mayburn that their son *wasn't* missing. But later he *was*."

"I always said those two boys spelled nothing but trouble."

The band played louder, marching closer, while the women talked on and on, as each newly arrived person added more information. Kids were yelling all around the park. The music was really loud. I recognized the final blasting strains of "Stars and Stripes Forever."

"Help," I yelled. "I'm up here!"

No one heard, or cared. Everyone was talking, yelling, cheering, tooting a trombone, or beating a drum.

"Here comes Mayor Puggett," someone said.

Things quieted down some. A husky throat was cleared, and someone who sounded as though he might be Mayor Eugene Puggett began to address the citizens of Siberia:

"Friends, neighbors, and my fellow residents of our fair community: As you know, today marks one more milestone in the history of our little hamlet. Today is Founder's Day, a day on which we all set aside our labors each year to pay a sincere and fervent tribute to a brave woman who was, according to our forefathers, the first settler to occupy this hallowed land."

I heard a scattering of applause. And then somebody yelled out: "Make it short and sweet, Eugene, on account you already been elected."

People laughed and Mayor Puggett again coughed to clear his gifted throat.

"And so," he continued, "it is my honor to invite you all to witness our Founder's Day pageant, directed by my able wife, directly following the event that we all gather here to see, the unveiling of our new statue of our first heroic citizen. This should be a happy day for us all, unmarked, unblemished, unfettered by sorrow. But yet sorrow has indeed struck our joyous community on what should be our most joyous day. The cruel stroke of Tragedy has struck one of our dear families. A lost child."

The crowd became silently sober.

"So," said Mayor Puggett, "permit me to ask all you out there in this audience to remove your hats as I now remove my own, and to bow our heads in a moment of silent prayer, asking the Almighty's help to return Finley Streeter to our midst."

I found myself, eyes closed, praying for my own safe return to my mother's loving arms.

"Surely," said Mayor Puggett after the silence, to cut all communication between Heaven and Siberia, "our prayers will be heard. More than just heard, they shall be answered."

"Amen," the crowd reverently mumbled.

"And now," said the mayor, "with sorrow misting our eyes and yet with hope abrim in all our hearts, I shall now unveil the centerpiece of our village green. The time has come. The moment arrives. Let the spirit of Samantha Brainlee Westcox be reborn in our eyes, thanks to the Stalwart Monument Company, that free of charge, offered to reface what the lashes of weather, not to mention a few pigeons, saw to deface."

The crowd was eagerly silent. Or bored.

"Friends," the mayor's voice rose to its full baritone,

"I give you . . . a new Samantha Brainlee Westcox, a sight you'll always remember."

Suddenly the ropes around me went slack. The covering was pulled away as sunlight stabbed into my squinting eyes. There was a gasp of dismay from the crowd, as though all the lungs of Siberia gulped greedily for enough oxygen to clear their boggled minds of the irreverent scene they now saw.

"The boy!" someone said.

"Ain't he the missing kid?"

"Whose boy *is* he?"

"Never you mind about that," laughed a man, "because I'd rather find out whose undershorts they be." The crowd tittered.

"What's going on?" whispered the mayor.

"That kid looks like he's about to pass out."

"Bring some water."

Frightened as I was, I could not seem to make my cramped arms let loose of the statue of Samantha. I just stood there, blinking at the sudden sunlight, wondering how badly I would be punished and by how many outraged people. The mayor, slightly confused himself, looked up and asked me a question:

"Are you the Dragavich kid?"

"Yes," I said.

"Well," said Mayor Puggett, "*you* ought to be thrashed good and proper. Ought to be ashamed of yourself, the way you showed disrespect for the whole town. You're under arrest."

I sort of wanted to cry.

"Say," said the mayor, "somebody go get Constable Hurley. Go fetch Mayburn."

Then I heard a voice that seemed far more calm than all of the others. It was my teacher, Mr. Little.

"That won't be necessary," he said. Mr. Little reached up to sort of hold on to me, as I felt a bit woozy. "Grab those shorts, Finley, and let's get out of here fast."

I heard a rip, and as I fell backward into the arms of Mr. Little, the lavender shorts came, too. Mr. Little hustled me through the crowd.

"Finley, I think I know where your parents are. And what's more, how glad they'll be to know you're safe and sound."

"Thanks a lot, Mr. Little."

chapter 12

"Finley!"

My mother's face was a welcome sight. I don't guess my spending the night tied to a statue had done either one of us much good. She looked worse than I felt. But she hugged me real hard.

"Safe and sound," said Mr. Little.

"Finley Streeter," said my mother, "you've turned all of Siberia upside down looking for you. We thought . . ."

". . . of the dam," said my father. "All right now, Finley, I want the truth and I want to hear it straight out."

"I think I can explain," said Mr. Little.

"This is my new teacher," I said quickly.

"You must be Mr. Little," said Pa.

"We've heard a lot about *you*," said my mother, "and the way you play the fiddle."

Pa said, "If this lad of ours ever gives you any trouble, Mr. Little, he'll quick sure wish he hadn't."

"Trouble?" said Mr. Little.

I held my breath. Here it comes, the whole story about *Hotsy Harem* and, on top of that, how Drag and I swiped his lavender underwear to hang on Samantha Brainlee Westcox. I closed my eyes and gritted my teeth because I knew darn well that Mr. Little was going to squeal on me and spill all the beans.

"No trouble at all," Mr. Little said. "In fact, I have an inkling that Finley and I are going to become real pals. For the rest of this year and all of next."

Pa looked at me as if he was fixing to ask why I was missing, where had I been, and what had I been up to. I was caught, cornered, and sinking fast. But then Mr. Little piped up and bailed me out.

"Come on, Finley," he said, "or we'll *never* be ready for the pageant. Hope you folks'll excuse us. I have to play the fiddle and your son has to be an Indian. Good to meet you people."

Before either Ma or Pa could crank up more questions, Mr. Little grabbed my arm hard and hauled me off at a trot.

"You're really okay, Mr. Little," I told him.

His eyebrows raised as he looked at me. "Why thank you, Finley. You'll never know how highly I value your approval." And then he smiled his gentle little smile, the one that sort of said he wasn't too doggone serious.

We found Drag.

Or rather Mr. Little found him hiding in the bushes, looking as though he didn't know whether he'd be a jailbird or an Indian.

"Come on, Stanley," said Mr. Little. "I know a nifty place to hide. If you're interested."

"Where?" asked Drag.

Five minutes later, Mr. Little was smearing Indian paint on our faces. Half the kids in school were wearing it and Mr. Little was right. Behind our streaks and blotches of red and yellow warpaint was one heck of a hiding place. All of us looked alike. Even my own parents wouldn't have recognized me and that seemed like a good idea, considering the trouble that Drag and I had gotten into.

We saw Miss Kellogg!

She was finally here, hugging everyone, and prettier than ever. I knew that she couldn't marry *me*, but I hoped the guy she did marry loved her even more than I did. She was already in costume for the pageant, and I don't guess even Samantha Brainlee Westcox ever looked more beautiful than Miss K.

"Miss Kellogg," I said, "there's somebody that you just *have* to meet."

"Who?" she asked.

"Somebody real special," I said. "Miss Kellogg, may I present the best teacher in the whole town of Siberia. This here is Mr. Little."

"Yeah," said Drag, "and that goes double for me."

"What a pleasure," said Mr. Little as he shook hands with Miss Kellogg. "I'm afraid Room 4 will never be the same without you, Miss Kellogg. Excuse me, but I don't believe I recall your married name."

"I'm now Mrs. Anderson," said Miss Kellogg, "and I've heard wonderful things about you, Mr. Little, and your fiddle."

"Places!" Mrs. Puggett blew her whistle and was yelling into her little megaphone. "Everybody, please be in position. The curtain's going up."

Needless to say, there wasn't any curtain around the millpond, but somehow the settlers settled around the campfire and began to sing their song. That was when the musket went off, by accident, which prompted Drag and me to run forward, way ahead of schedule, so that he could "die." So as Drag stumbled forward, faking his agony, all the rest of us who were Indians ran forward, too. Out of the ambushes.

Miss O'Leary played the piano, Mr. Little played the fiddle, swelling the music to a peak of excitement, as Samantha Brainlee Westcox (played by Miss Kellogg who was now Mrs. Anderson) jumped on Mr. Epstein's raft and headed for safety. Only then did our Indian chief, Constable Mayburn Hurley, arrive, smeared with fifty pounds of cocoa powder and face paint. He looked at Drag, who was still "dying," and asked me:

"What's wrong with that kid?"

The crowd cheered, possibly because Mayburn Hurley was the largest and funniest Indian in Siberia, or because Samantha made her escape from the massacre to safety. Kids were now enjoying the general hysteria, running all over the shoreline of the millpond. I was "tomahawking" Stewy Ordway and having a dandy old time.

The band played.

I guess they figured that they might as well, because the wind had come up, and the sound of one fiddle and one piano drained away. Mrs. Puggett was blowing her whistle and trying to collect us all together to make our bow to the audience, but nobody seemed to pay too much mind. Drag and I were doing our best to stay in back of Mayburn Hurley so he wouldn't recall the prank we'd played with a statue and some underwear.

Somewhere, from the center of the crowd, I heard my mother calling "Finley!" but I pretended not to hear. Mrs. Dragavich was also hollering to her "Stanley!" but Drag wasn't about to listen. I don't guess either one of us wanted to join our parents until they had plenty of time to cool their collars. Pa's face had been a bit more ruddy than usual this morning, and I sure didn't hanker to start answering questions—the kind of answers that amounted to either a fib or a flailing. Probable a parcel of both.

The wind had really come up, and a few early autumn leaves blew down from the trees and into the water, as though to remind Siberia that October wasn't too far away. It sure was gusty. Some of the ladies in the crowd hung on to their skirts, and I saw a man put a hand on a hat.

Then I spotted Mr. Little! I couldn't believe what I

·saw. He was running along the shoreline toward the dam, faster than I would have believed he could run. And then I suddenly saw why:

The wind was blowing the raft toward the dam!

Miss Kellogg had probably been out there on the water, yelling for help, but nobody heard her, because of all of the music and cheering and wind.

"She's going over the edge," said Drag.

In one second, everyone in Siberia was silently and helplessly watching the raft blow toward the top of the waterfall. Miss Kellogg was waving; and even from afar off, I could read the fright on her face.

"Jump!" people hollered.

"Won't do no good," a man said. "The wind's whipped up the current. It'll suck her right over."

People started to scream. One of the Volunteer Fire Department men ran toward Siberia's big red fire-truck. He and another fireman grabbed a coil of rope.

"Look!"

I saw Mr. Little running along the catwalk that led to the dam. It was no place to run, as below him was a long fall into a mess of ugly rocks. Yet he ran. I saw his small body, clothes and all, dive out over the lip of the dam. I saw the raft go over the edge where it would smash to bits on the rocks. Just to look down into that white churning water was scary enough.

Before hitting the water, Mr. Little's arm swept Miss Kellogg off the raft. Both of them splashed into the millpond. I watched two heads go under.

They didn't come up.

chapter 13

It was Thursday.

And that morning, not one single kid in all of Siberia Central School was late. We were early, in order to cheer like crazy when we saw Mr. Little coming to school from the direction of Mrs. Tripper's Boarding House.

"Hooray!" we yelled. And the closer he got to us, the better I could see him smile his gentle smile. There was a bandage on his hand.

"Three cheers for Mr. Little," a kid hollered.

Everyone crowded around him. We must have looked like a flock of baby chickens around a mother hen. Sometimes a boy or a girl reached a hand out, just to touch Mr. Little to see if he was real. Or was he steel, like Superman?

"He's *our* teacher," I said to Riley Evers, a kid in Miss Johnson's room.

"Yeah," said Drag, "and we're Room 4."

Finally we settled down and took our seats so Mr. Little could count up the attendance. Nobody was absent. Not on a day like today.

"You're a real hero, Mr. Little," I said, "and the whole town is talking about how you'd risk your own neck to save Miss Kellogg . . . I mean Mrs. Anderson."

Mr. Little smiled.

"How's your hand?" asked Drag.

"Tell us how you did it?" We all wanted to hear Mr. Little explain how he rescued Miss Kellogg just as she was about to wash over the falls.

Getting up from his desk, Mr. Little walked to the blackboard and drew sort of a diagram of the dam, with the deep millpond above it and the rocks beneath the falling water.

"Remember this," said Mr. Little, "in case you ever are caught in that current and you are about to wash over the falls: Your only chance is to stay deep. Don't try to fight the surface current. Instead, dive down deep, and then crab your way over to one side or another so you can grab a purchase on one of the catwalk pilings."

"Is that how you saved Miss Kellogg?"

Mr. Little nodded.

"A dam, like the one you people have in Siberia," he said, "is a place to stay away from. I swam in a millpond as a boy, and believe me, accidents always happen."

"Like the one yesterday," I said, "when the wind blew the raft."

"You're a real hero," said Drag. I could tell by the tone of his voice that he meant it.

I said, "You ought to get a medal, Mr. Little."

"No, I don't deserve a medal."

"But you're a *hero!* Don't you want to be a hero? Don't you even hanker to wear a medal on your chest?"

Mr. Little smiled. "Thank you, no."

"You could hang it up on your wall."

"Ah," said Mr. Little, "that reminds me." Reaching in his desk, he withdrew a picture of a man, which he hung on our classroom wall on a nail that was already hammered in.

"Who is it?" we asked.

"His name is Luigi Pirandello."

"Is he an American?"

"No, he's Italian."

"What's he do?"

"Many things," said Mr. Little. "He is a gifted man. A poet, an author of books, a writer of plays, and a few short stories."

"*I* never heard of him," said Drag.

"Nor," said Mr. Little with a wink, "has *he* ever heard of you."

We all laughed, even Drag.

We talked a lot that morning about Mr. Luigi Pirandello and some of the things he did as a student. Sometimes, according to Mr. Little, Mr. Pirandello hated his teachers and got himself in trouble.

At recess, everyone went out to play, except for Drag and me.

"Mr. Little . . ."

"Yes?"

"We're sorry," I said.

Drag said, "We did it. Us two."

"I know," said Mr. Little.

"Aren't ya mad?" asked Drag.

Mr. Little reached out his hands, even though one wore a bandage, to touch us both very lightly on the shoulders. "Boys," he said, "let me advise you on the subject of losing one's temper. Rage is perhaps the least useful of all our many feelings. To hate somebody usually will hurt *you* more than it will ever hurt your particular enemy."

Drag and I nodded.

"To tell you the truth," Mr. Little went on, "I was amused by your prank, the magazine you hid inside my umbrella."

"You were?"

"Indeed. It was rather creative."

"You're not sore?" asked Drag.

"Not a bit. Somebody once said, I think it might have been President Lincoln, that you can tell the size of a man by the size of the thing that makes him mad."

"I like that," I said.

"We swiped your undershorts," said Drag, "so Fin and I will pay you back the money to buy a new pair."

"Fair enough," said Mr. Little. "And again, let me say *that* was a darn good prank, too. Very inventive."

"It was?"

"Quite. Yet always be careful when you're up to mischief."

"You mean . . . don't get caught."

"No," said Mr. Little, "not that. What I mean is, when you are about to play a trick on somebody, be sure that what you do is fun, even for your victim."

"How come?"

"Well, because it just isn't very brave to take your pleasure at the expense of some other guy's pain. That's what cowards do. You see, a bully is a sissy. Because a bully never picks a fight with a strong kid. Only with a kid who is weaker."

I was listening, and more, I was starting to like Mr. Little a whole lot. So I put my hand up on his shoulder.

"If you both will allow me," he said, "rather than just being your teacher, I would be honored to also be your friend."

"*Sure!*" said Drag.

"We won't play any more pranks on you, sir," I said straight out.

Mr. Little scowled. "Please don't tell me *that*, Finley, as my life in Siberia could be quite dull unless I kept myself constantly on my toes."

"Gee," said Drag, "I never thought I'd have a hero for a teacher. You really got guts, Mr. Little. You sure do."

"It must take a lot of guts to be a hero," I said. "Does it?"

Mr. Little looked at the picture of Luigi Pirandello.

"Boys, I suppose it does take courage to be a hero. But it takes so much *more* courage . . . to be a gentleman."

About the Author

ROBERT NEWTON PECK comes from a long line of Vermont farmers. At the age of seventeen, during World War II, he joined the 88th Infantry Division and after the war returned home to attend Rollins College. Although a prolific writer, author of the enormously popular *A Day No Pigs Would Die,* Mr. Peck has not limited himself to purely literary pursuits. He is an enthusiastic public speaker, has killed hogs, worked in a paper mill, and made his living as a lumberjack. In his spare time he enjoys playing ragtime piano and the old Scottish game of curling.

He lives in Longwood, Florida.